The Christmas Cats in Silly Hats

By Connie Corcoran Wilson

Original Artwork by:
Andrew Weinert
and
Emily K. Marquez

Quad City Press 2011

Quad City Press
2127 3rd. Street B
East Moline, IL 61244-2409

Also by Connie Corcoran Wilson

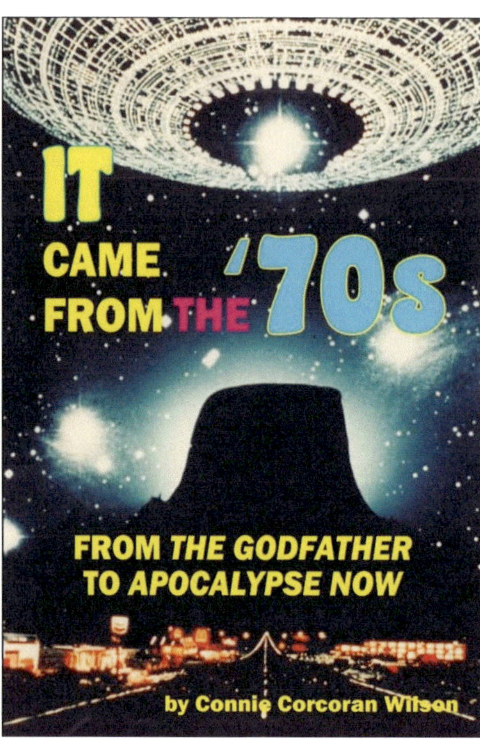

Ebook Only

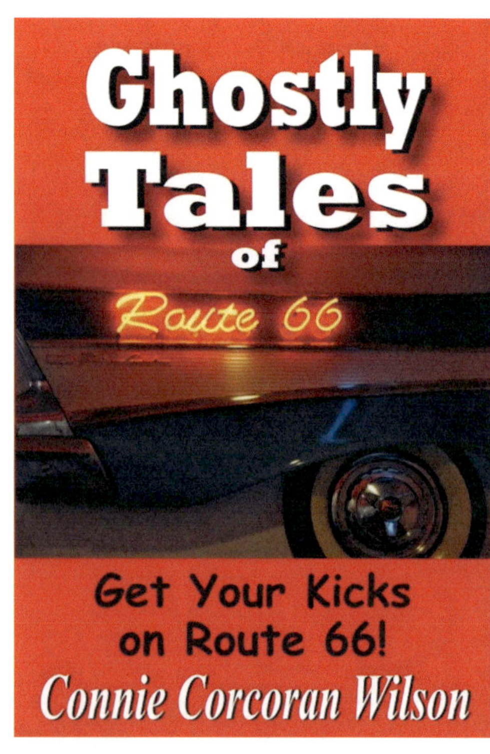

Dedication

This book is dedicated to Emily Marquez of Bejuma, Venezuela, who cared for Ava and Elise Wilson in Chicago as an au pair when the girls were 2 to 3 years old. Emily provided additional drawings for Andy Weinert's original artwork, when the book morphed into a Christmas book for the girls, a gift from Emily and Nanna Connie.

Emily has been a real treasure. The girls are bilingual (at only 2 years of age as of this writing) as a result of her efforts (Spanish and English), and her artwork has greatly enhanced this project, adding to Andy Weinert's original drawings.

We will all miss Emily very, very much when she leaves for her next adventure in China, and we all wish her much, much success and happiness in the future, wherever it leads her.

Christmas cats
in silly hats.

They never know
where they are at.

These two aren't
the best of friends.

They like to fight
o'er odds and ends.

Both are crazy,
in a way.

Dressing up
from day to day.

One cat thinks
he is a King.
(That cat doesn't
know a thing.)

8

Both cats like to
chase bluebirds.
Both cats argue:
they meow words.
It's quite clear
they'll have to be
better friends -
like you and me.

One cat lurks

inside a box.

12

One cat plays
inside my socks.

One will not share.
And that is bad.

It makes the
other cat so mad!

They fight
through screens.

They both
act mean.

Both cats race around the house.

Both will always chase a mouse.

One cat thinks he's World's Best Cook.

But that's not the story of this book.

One cat likes
to put out flames.
But that cat
also always blames
the other cat
for fights. (For shame!)
Their fights are
really, really lame.

Finally, they learned
to get along.

Became great friends
in story and song.

The Christmas cats in silly hats learned to share and that was that.

The Christmas
cats in silly hats
gave up their petty,
catty spats.

They learned to
get along so well,
their happy tale
I'm here to tell.

28
Merry Christmas!
He's my best friend.
The End

About the Author

Connie (Corcoran) Wilson (MS + 30) graduated from the University of Iowa and Western Illinois University, with additional study at Northern Illinois, the University of California at Berkeley and the University of Chicago. She taught writing at six Iowa/Illinois colleges and has written for five newspapers and seven blogs, including Associated Content (now owned by Yahoo) which named her its 2008 Content Producer of the Year . She is an active, voting member of HWA (Horror Writers Association).

Her stories and interviews with writers like David Morrell, Joe Hill, Kurt Vonnegut, William F. Nolan, Frederik Pohl and Anne Perry have appeared online and in numerous journals. Her work has won prizes from "Whim's Place Flash Fiction," "Writer's Digest" (Screenplay) and she will have 12 books out by the end of the year. Connie reviewed film and books for the Quad City Times (Davenport, Iowa) for 12 years and wrote humor columns and conducted interviews for the (Moline, Illinois) Daily Dispatch and now blogs for 7 blogs, including television reviews and political reporting for Yahoo.

Connie lives in East Moline, Illinois with husband Craig and cat Lucy, and in Chicago, Illinois, where her son, Scott and daughter-in-law Jessica and their two-year-old twins Elise and Ava reside. Her daughter, Stacey, recently graduated from Belmont University in Nashville, Tennessee, as a Music Business graduate.

Made in the USA
Monee, IL
07 July 2026

56552405R00021